Dolphin
School

Echo's
New Pet

Dolphin School

Echo's New Pet

by Catherine Hapka
illustrated by Hollie Hibbert

SCHOLASTIC INC.

ISBN 978-1-338-05374-6

10 9 8 7 6 5 4 3 2 1   16 17 18 19 20

Printed in the U.S.A.   40
First printing, September 2016
Book design by Jennifer Rinaldi Windau

1

Old Salty's Assignment

"WELCOME, STUDENTS," OLD SALTY CALLED out. "Quiet down, please. We have something very exciting to talk about in class today."

Pearl's friend Echo giggled softly. "I doubt that," she whispered. "He'll probably just talk about barnacles, like he did yesterday."

Pearl smiled and nudged Echo with her fin. "*Shh*," she said. "You don't want him to hear you."

Old Salty was the principal of Coral Cove Dolphin School. He also taught Ocean Lore class to all the first-year students, including Pearl and her friends.

Pearl loved all her classes, but she had to admit that Ocean Lore could be boring. Especially when Old Salty decided to talk in great detail about barnacles or algae.

Pearl's friends Flip and Splash were floating nearby. "What's so exciting about the life cycle of barnacles?" Flip called out. "Isn't that what we're learning more about today?"

Old Salty chuckled, causing bubbles to pour out of his blowhole. "I'm afraid our friends the barnacles shall have to wait for another day. Today I have a special assignment for you."

"A special assignment?" Splash did a quick flip, sending a passing school of damselfish scattering for safety. The school was encircled by a large coral reef, which meant there were always lots of fish and other creatures swimming around with the dolphins. "What is it?"

"I'm about to tell you." The teacher smiled. "Tomorrow we will be having Show and Tell."

Everyone started whispering excitedly around Pearl. She heard Wiggle, one of the other dolphins in the class, whisper, "What's Show and Tell?"

"My brother told me about Show and Tell!" Splash called out. "Last year he brought in a huge fireworm. He found it on the reef near where my pod lives."

A pod is a dolphin family. Pearl knew that there were about twenty dolphins in Splash's pod. Echo and Flip lived in an even larger pod. It consisted of more than fifty dolphins! Pearl's pod was much smaller. It had just four members—Pearl, her parents, and her little sister, Squeak.

"Yes, I remember that fireworm," Old Salty told Splash. "It was a fine specimen indeed."

Pearl's mind was racing. "Wait," she called out. "Do you mean we all need to find worms to bring in?"

"Not at all," the teacher replied. "Show and Tell is all about learning more about the ocean around us. You may bring whatever sort of object or creature you like, as long as it's something we might study in this class. That could include interesting shells, seaweed, oddly colored sand or stones, barnacles . . ."

"I wonder if we'd get extra credit for bringing in a barnacle," Flip whispered to Pearl. "They're Old Salty's favorite!"

Old Salty was still talking. ". . . and, of

course, some students can choose to use their other dolphin skills to convince a pretty fish or fascinating crustacean to come to school with them for the day."

Pearl nodded. As protectors of the ocean, all dolphins had natural magic abilities. One of the things they used magic for was communicating with the other creatures who lived in the Salty Sea.

"I know a cool pipefish I could bring," one of the other students called out. Her name was Bubbles, and she was always cheerful. "How long would he have to stay?"

"Just through your first class period," Old Salty said. "That's when the entire school will gather to see what you first years have brought in for Show and Tell. We'll all learn and experience it together."

The whole school? Pearl blew out a nervous burst of bubbles.

Splash didn't seem nervous at all. He was spinning in circles with excitement. "Wow, this is cool!" he exclaimed. "I wonder what I should bring!"

"Don't worry about it too much," Flip said. "Because my Show and Tell is going to be the best one the school has ever seen!"

Echo snorted out a trail of bubbles. "Stop bragging, Flip," she said.

"It's not bragging if it's true," Flip bragged.

Pearl didn't pay much attention to their bickering. She was too busy trying to figure out what she could bring tomorrow!

Pearl was still thinking about Old Salty's assignment when class ended. "What do you think you'll bring in for Show and Tell?" she asked her friends as they swam across the cove.

"Something great," Flip said right away.

"But not as great as what I bring," Echo countered.

Splash laughed. "I can't wait to see what you two bring in. Now come on, we don't want to be late for Magic!"

Magic class took place near the kelp forest at

one end of the school cove. Their teacher, Bay, was already waiting there when the students swam in.

Pearl said hello to Bay. So did Splash, Wiggle, Bubbles, and the others.

But Echo and Flip were still arguing. "What are you going to do, bring a whale into dolphin school?!" Echo said with a snort.

"Maybe." Flip smirked. "Or maybe I'll catch a Land Legger!"

"Are you talking about Show and Tell?" Bay asked with a smile. "I have to admit, nobody has ever brought in a Land Legger before."

Pearl giggled along with the rest of the class. Land Leggers lived on the islands and shorelines above the surface of the sea. Pearl had never even seen one up close.

"I was just kidding about the Land Legger,"

Flip admitted. "But I'm going to bring in something super great—you'll see!"

"All right." Bay swam to the center of the group. "Enough about that for now. We have a lot to do today." She sent out a burst of magic energy. A moment later a large eel swam into view from among the waving strands of kelp.

"Ooh, a conger eel!" Splash did an excited spin. "Cool!"

Bay explained that the students would be practicing their guiding today. Guiding was a basic magical skill. It was a way of convincing other creatures to do something. Eels, fish, and most other animals in the sea couldn't talk like dolphins could, but they could understand simple feelings, ideas, and images. Guiding was sending ideas or feelings to another creature. Dolphins could use guiding to do things, like convincing a fish to move in a certain direction or asking a crab or shrimp to stay still.

"I want you to try guiding this eel to swim over to the reef wall and back," Bay explained. "It might not be easy. Conger eels are much more challenging to guide than some other creatures. Now, who wants to go first?"

"I will." Echo waved her fin.

Pearl wasn't surprised that her friend had volunteered. Echo's mother had especially strong magic, and so did Echo.

Pearl and the others watched Echo swim closer to the eel. "Go, Echo!" Splash whispered, doing several flips in a row.

Echo sent out a burst of magical energy. Pearl waited for the eel to turn and swim toward the reef.

But instead, he turned the other way—and swam toward Splash!

"Hey," Echo called to the eel. "Wrong way!"

She sent out more magical energy. Several passing fish felt it and swam toward the reef.

But not the eel. Instead, he followed Splash up toward the surface.

Splash took a breath, then did a flip on his way back down. "Sorry, Echo," he said. "I guess he likes me!"

Echo looked annoyed. But Bay chuckled. "In that case, why don't you give it a try next?" she told Splash.

"Sure. Here goes nothing." Splash laughed, and so did most of the other students. Everyone knew that Splash wasn't very good at magic. He was much better at his favorite class, Jumping and Swimming.

"Come on, buddy," Splash told the eel, sending out a burst of magical energy. "Let's go!" He zipped closer to the reef, still sending his message.

The eel stared at him for a moment. Then he swam toward the reef and back again.

"Yay, Splash!" Flip cheered. "You got it on the first try!"

Splash looked surprised. "Wow, I did!"

Pearl was a little surprised, too. Normally Splash was too restless and excitable to do well at solo guiding.

"Good job, Splash." Bay smiled. "Who's next?"

Flip volunteered. Pearl noticed that Echo looked dejected.

"Don't worry," Pearl whispered, swimming closer and rubbing her friend's fin. "Like Bay said, eels are challenging."

Echo frowned. "So why did Splash get it on his first try?"

"Old Salty told us the other day that conger eels are attracted to movement, remember?" Pearl smiled. "And Splash always has plenty of that!"

Echo smiled, too, but she still didn't look very happy. Pearl guessed it was because she was used to being the best at everything magical.

"You'll get it next time," Pearl whispered. "Don't worry!"

2

What to Bring?

THAT AFTERNOON, PEARL SWAM HOME AS quickly as she could. She was eager to tell her parents and sister about Show and Tell.

"Pearl!" Squeak yelled when Pearl swam into the quiet lagoon where their pod lived. "Look, more baby turtles hatched today!"

She waved a fin at several tiny hatchlings swimming around in the shallows. The sea turtles were the reason Pearl's pod lived in that lagoon. The grown-up turtles returned every year to lay their eggs on the beach. When the babies hatched a couple of months later, Pearl's family helped them find their way safely out to sea.

Pearl smiled. She loved hatching season! "Hello," she greeted the baby turtles. "It's nice to meet you. Welcome to the Salty Sea!"

Most of the baby turtles kept swimming around without paying much attention to Pearl. But the smallest one swam over and stared at Pearl with big, curious, dark eyes.

Squeak giggled. "I call that one Nosy," she told Pearl. "He seems really interested in everything and keeps bumping me with his nose when he wants to play."

"Hi, Nosy." Pearl laughed as the turtle bumped her on the snout. He was so cute!

"Let's teach him to play tag," Squeak suggested.

"In a minute," Pearl said. "Where are Mom and Dad? I have something exciting to tell you guys."

She found her parents in the surf near the beach. Her mother was peering at the sandy shore where the turtles laid their eggs.

"I expect more will hatch tonight," she was saying when Pearl and Squeak swam over.

Pearl's father nodded, then noticed his children. "Welcome home, Pearl," he said, rubbing her fin with his own. "Squeak, how are the new babies doing?"

"Fine," Squeak said. "Especially Nosy. He never stops moving!"

Just then Pearl felt something bump her fluke. She spun around in surprise and saw Nosy right behind her.

Squeak saw him, too. "See what I mean?" she told her parents with a giggle.

"Never mind that." Pearl smiled at the baby turtle, then returned her attention to her family. "I need your help!"

As they all swam back out into deeper water, she told them about Show and Tell. "I see," her mother said when she finished. "Do you have any ideas about what to bring, Pearl?"

"Not really." Pearl looked around the quiet lagoon. "Old Salty says we can bring anything, but I want to bring something cool. What about a giant squid?"

Squeak giggled, sending tiny bubbles floating up toward the surface. "There are no giant squid around here, silly."

"I guess you're right." Pearl spotted a pretty, wavy-edged shell. "Maybe I could find a really big oyster."

"Or an oyster with a pearl in it!" Squeak sounded excited. "That would be cool, especially since your name is Pearl."

"It might be hard to find a pearl by tomorrow." Pearl flicked her fluke while she tried to think of other ideas. Then she felt it bump against something.

"Careful!" her father said. "Nosy is trying to play with your tail."

Pearl laughed and turned to touch the tiny

turtle with her snout. "Sorry, Nosy," she said. "I didn't mean to bump into you."

Nosy didn't seem upset. He flapped his flippers as he chased after Pearl's tail again.

"He sure does like to play," Pearl's mother said with a smile.

Pearl's father nodded. "I bet he'd like to visit Coral Cove Dolphin School, too."

"What do you mean?" Pearl asked. She was still trying to think of a good item to bring for Show and Tell. Could she convince the cranky old octopus who lived in her lagoon to go to school with her? Or maybe she could find an extra-pretty tulip shell . . .

"Your father is right," her mother said. "Pearl, why don't you bring Nosy to Show and Tell?"

"That's a great idea, Pearlie!" Squeak did a flip.

"But he's just a sea turtle," Pearl said. She stared at Nosy, who had just swum down to sniff at a shell on the lagoon's sandy floor.

"I bet he would love to go with you," Squeak said. "Right, Nosy?"

Pearl felt a burst of magical energy coming from her little sister. Most dolphins didn't learn much about sending mental messages to other species until they went to school, and Squeak was too young for school. But both she and Pearl had learned the basics about communicating with sea turtles when they were young. That way they could help their parents take care of the babies.

Nosy blinked at Squeak. Then he swam over and bumped Pearl's face, letting out an excited chirp at the same time.

Pearl wasn't sure what to say. She was

supposed to bring something interesting to show the whole school. Nosy was cute . . . but was a baby sea turtle exciting enough?

Her father was watching her. "I know the turtles are like family to us, Pearl," he said. "But most dolphins don't get to see sea turtles very often—especially hatchlings. I think your classmates would find Nosy very interesting."

Pearl wasn't sure about that. But she decided not to worry about what the whole school thought. She didn't need to be the best. She was always telling her friends about the turtles in her lagoon, and now she had a chance to share the real thing with them!

"Okay," she said, smiling at Nosy. "What do you say, little guy? Want to come to school with me tomorrow?"

She focused her magic, sending a mental

message to the little turtle. It showed the two of them swimming toward the large, beautiful coral reef that formed the walls of the school.

Nosy stared at her with wide, curious eyes. Then a quick, blurry image popped into Pearl's mind—it showed Nosy leading the way toward the reef!

"He said yes!" she told her family with a smile. "I guess that means I found my Show and Tell!"

Several more baby turtles hatched that night. By morning, there were at least a dozen of the tiny creatures swimming around. They tasted the seaweed growing in the lagoon, chased one another around, and dove down to send up spurts of sand. For a second Pearl wished she didn't have to leave them to go to school.

Then she remembered: Today was Show and Tell!

"Where's Nosy?" Pearl asked her little sister. "I don't see him."

"I'm not sure." Squeak swam closer to the young turtles. "Nosy, where are you?"

Several hatchlings swam over. But Pearl still didn't see Nosy.

"I hope he didn't leave the lagoon." Squeak sent out a worried burst of bubbles. "Let's look out by the reef."

Pearl's lagoon was sheltered by two craggy coral formations. Beyond that, the water got much deeper.

"There's one!" Pearl pointed a fin at a tiny turtle nibbling on a plant near the coral. "Is it Nosy?"

"Let's see." But when the dolphins swam

closer, the little turtle spotted them—and dashed out of sight behind a clump of seaweed!

"Hey!" Squeak exclaimed. "Nosy, it's us! Don't be scared."

Nosy peered out from behind the seaweed. An image floated into Pearl's mind—the baby turtle hiding from a group of huge, scary dolphins with teeth like sharks.

Squeak looked at her sister. "I think he's scared to go to school."

"Oh no." Pearl's heart sank. What would she do if Nosy didn't want to be her Show and Tell project after all? "Nosy, don't be scared! You can trust me—I'm your friend. And I'll be with you the whole time."

Nosy blinked at her. Then he darted out and bumped her with his nose. This time a happy, excited feeling floated into Pearl's mind.

She smiled with relief. "Great! Now let's get going—we're already late!"

Nosy couldn't swim as fast as a dolphin, so it took Pearl longer than usual to get to school. By the time she swam into the cove, most of the students and teachers were already gathered in the open area at the center of the school lagoon.

"Sorry I'm late," she told Bay breathlessly as she swam past. "I had to convince Nosy to come with me."

"Ah, a baby sea turtle?" Bay said with a smile. "How interesting!"

Pearl smiled back. Bay was so nice! That was one of the reasons why she was Pearl's favorite teacher.

Then Pearl spotted her friends near the front of the group. She swam toward them.

"Excuse me," she said as she passed a group of older students. One of them was Splash's older brother, Finny. He was floating beside his friends Mullet and Shelly.

Shelly let out a burst of bubbles when she saw Nosy. "Ooh, what a cute little guy!" she cooed.

"Thanks." Pearl smiled at her. "Come on, Nosy, over here!"

Nosy pressed against her, staring around with wide, slightly nervous eyes. But he let out a chirp and followed Pearl as she headed over to join her friends.

She reached them just as Old Salty let out a whistle for attention. "All right, students!" he announced. "It's time for Show and Tell!"

3

Show and Tell

"HI," PEARL WHISPERED TO HER FRIENDS AS Old Salty said a few more words about Show and Tell. "Sorry I'm late. What did you guys bring?"

"You'll see in a second." Echo didn't even glance at Nosy. She was floating above a large, pretty seashell. "I'll go first!" she called out when Old Salty asked for a volunteer.

Pearl watched with interest as her friend nudged the shell forward. Then Echo turned and smiled at the crowd.

"I brought a conch shell for Show and Tell,"

she said proudly. "It's the biggest one I've ever seen! It was empty when I found it. But you can see that it once belonged to a queen conch. Isn't the pink color pretty?"

She talked about conchs a little more, then looked over at Old Salty.

"Very nice, Echo," the teacher said, swimming over to examine the conch shell. "It's a fine specimen."

"Thanks." Echo floated there for a few more seconds, as if waiting for him to say something else about the conch.

Instead, Old Salty looked at the crowd. "All right, who's next?"

"Me! Me!" Flip darted forward before anyone else could volunteer. Pearl had been so busy watching Echo's presentation that she hadn't noticed what her other friends had brought. But now she saw that Flip had an enormous red cushion sea star.

"Wow!" she said to Splash and Echo. "That's the biggest sea star I've ever seen!"

All around the cove, other students were oohing and aahing over the size of the creature as well. Flip looked pleased.

"It's huge, right?" he said, puffing up his chest with pride. "Sea stars like this one usually only have five arms. But check it out—this one has seven! Isn't that cool?"

He kept talking for a few more minutes. At the end of his presentation, Flip brought the sea star back over to Pearl and the others. "Good job, buddy," Splash said, giving Flip a high five with his fin.

Echo didn't look that impressed. "Big deal," she muttered. "There are sea stars all over the place. Look, there are three of them on the coral right over there."

Pearl glanced at the nearest section of the reef. She was surprised that Echo sounded so grouchy. Was it because she thought Flip's Show and Tell was better than hers?

Probably, Pearl thought. *Echo likes to be the best at everything.*

Several other students gave their

presentations. Bubbles had brought the pipefish she'd mentioned. A dolphin named Harmony's item was a pretty blue parrot fish. A student from the other first-year school pod had convinced a jellyfish to accompany her. The presentations were so interesting that Pearl didn't have a chance to get nervous.

Then it was Splash's turn. "Wish me luck," he whispered to Pearl and the others when Old Salty called his name. "I forgot to find something yesterday. I thought I'd just have to grab a fish from the school reef or something!" He laughed. "But luckily I found this on the way to school."

He swam forward with his item, a weirdly shaped clear object. "What is that thing?" Pearl wondered.

"Shh," Flip said. "He's going to tell us."

"I brought this," Splash told the audience. "It used to belong to a Land Legger. At least I think it did."

Old Salty swam forward for a closer look. "Yes, I've seen such things before," he said. "Land Leggers often drop them into the sea near their beaches when they don't want them anymore."

"That's right." This time Riptide came forward. He was the Jumping and Swimming teacher. "A friend of mine lived with Land Leggers for a while. He said they suck on such things frequently." Riptide shrugged. "Perhaps these items help them breathe?"

"Wow," Flip said. "Cool!"

"Yes, fascinating." Old Salty smiled at Splash, then peered out at the rest of the group. "Who wants to go next? How about you, Pearl?"

Pearl felt a flutter of nervousness as she swam forward. She was so nervous that she forgot to tell Nosy it was their turn. Luckily, the little sea turtle followed her to the front of the group.

"Hi," Pearl said, sending up a little flurry of bubbles. "Um, this is Nosy. He's a baby sea turtle. He just hatched a couple of nights ago."

Pearl heard a few oohs and aahs. A third-year student named Grayfin even swam a little closer.

"He's so tiny and adorable!" she exclaimed.

"I know, right?" Shelly said. "How'd you find him, Pearl?"

"My pod lives in a lagoon where the turtles hatch every year," Pearl explained.

"Really?" Splash's brother called out. "That's amazing!"

"I guess so." Pearl smiled at Nosy, feeling a little more confident now that everyone seemed so interested. "To me, it's just home."

"How many baby turtles hatch each year?" someone called out.

"Do they hatch every night?" someone else asked.

"Are they all that small?"

Pearl swam up to the surface for a breath. Nosy followed, staying close behind her as she returned.

Finny laughed. "Aw, look," she called out. "He's sticking to Pearl like a remora following a shark!"

That made everyone laugh, including Pearl. "All right, settle down," Bay called out. "Pearl? Why don't you tell us all more about your little friend?"

Pearl did her best, explaining how the mother turtles came back every year to lay their eggs, and how her family helped the babies find their way out to sea. While she was talking, Nosy grew bolder. He swam around doing circles and dives. Then he darted over to nibble at the seaweed another student had brought. When she shooed him away, Nosy chirped and sped over to bite at a stalk of algae instead.

Pearl kept one eye on Nosy while she talked. She was proud of him for being so brave.

Finally she finished answering everyone's questions. "Come on, Nosy," she called to the baby turtle, who was zipping around happily. "It's time for someone else to have a turn."

She guided the hatchling to follow her back over to her friends.

"Great presentation, Pearl!" Flip said, touching her fin with his.

"Yeah, awesome!" Splash did a flip.

"Thanks." Pearl looked at Echo to see what she thought. But Echo was staring at Old Salty and didn't say anything.

Pearl was surprised. Normally Echo said

something nice when Pearl did well in school, just like Pearl had complimented Echo's presentation earlier. That was what friends did—right?

Oh well, Pearl thought, shooting Echo one more look. *Maybe she's just eager to hear the next presentation.*

She turned to listen as another student swam to the front for his turn. Finding out what Echo thought of Nosy would just have to wait until Show and Tell was over.

4

Echo's Idea

"THAT'S ALL, FOLKS," OLD SALTY SAID AS THE last student finished his talk about the sea urchin he'd brought for Show and Tell. "Great job, first years! You all found very interesting items."

Bay nodded as she swam over to join him. "Everyone can now go to their second-period classes."

Pearl was a little disappointed that she'd missed her first class of the day, Music. It was one of her favorites. Still, Show and Tell had been fun!

"I'll race you to Jumping and Swimming," Splash said.

"No way," Pearl said with a laugh. "Nosy will never be able to keep up!"

Most of the students who'd brought live creatures had let them go right after Show and Tell. But Nosy was too young to find his way back to the lagoon alone, so he was staying with Pearl all day.

"Oops, I forgot." Splash smiled sheepishly at the tiny turtle. "Don't worry, little buddy. We'll go at your speed."

Flip watched Nosy chase a passing fish with a happy chirp. "That turtle is really cool, Pearl," he said. "Maybe even almost as cool as my sea star."

"You guys go ahead to class without me," Echo said. "I need to talk to Old Salty about whether my conch shell is the largest he's ever seen."

"Are you sure?" Pearl began. "We can wait, if you . . ."

She let her voice trail off. Echo had already dashed off with her conch.

"We'd better go," Flip said. "Riptide doesn't like it when we're late."

Pearl wanted to wait for Echo. But the boys were right—Riptide could be strict. And Pearl wasn't very good at Jumping and Swimming

to begin with. She definitely didn't want to make the teacher mad. So she followed Flip and Splash toward the cove entrance.

Jumping and Swimming class usually took place outside the reef. The water was a little deeper there, though not as deep as it was a few minutes' swim away in Bigsky Basin. Most dolphins avoided Bigsky Basin, since large sharks sometimes swam through there.

"Shake a fin, students," Riptide called out. "We have a lot to do today."

"I hope Echo gets here soon," Pearl whispered to the boys. "Riptide will yell at her if she's late."

"There she is." Flip waved his fluke toward the school.

Echo had just emerged. She swam over and joined the group. Pearl wanted to ask her friend what Old Salty had said about the conch. But she was afraid to talk when Riptide was giving instructions, so she decided to wait until later.

"Show and Tell was fun," Riptide said, swimming back and forth in front of the group. "But now it's time to get back to work."

"Cool!" Splash said, doing three flips in a row.

Riptide chuckled. "Good attitude, Splash!" he barked out. "You can help me demonstrate our next exercise."

"Okay, what should I do?" Splash swam forward eagerly.

The baby sea turtle scooted right after Splash! "Nosy, stop!" Pearl whispered. But there wasn't enough time to guide the hatchling back to her side, so she grabbed his tail with her snout. Nosy chirped in annoyance.

Riptide glanced over. "Who's that?" he said. Swimming closer, he smiled. "Oh, I see. Welcome to class, little fella!"

Nosy stared at him in awe. Then he let out a happy chirp and swam in a circle.

Riptide chuckled. "All right, back to work…" He told the class that today they would be working on moving objects. He'd noticed that some of the dolphins had had trouble moving their Show and Tell items around.

"Try this," he told Splash. "Swim down and grab one of those stones. Scoop it up with your snout and flip it up through the water. See how high you can get it to go."

Pearl looked down. The seafloor was littered with large, smooth stones of many colors.

Splash nodded and did as Riptide said. He zipped down, scooped up a pretty gray stone, and flipped it up. The stone tumbled up through the water—almost to the surface!

"Excellent!" Riptide roared. "Now everyone give it a try."

Pearl swam forward with the others. She spotted a small white stone and swam toward it. But Nosy zipped in front of her, and she almost crashed into him.

"Careful, Nosy," she warned. "You need to stay out of the way."

But the tiny turtle was staring at Echo. He chirped and swam toward her.

Once again, there was no time to guide him with magic. Instead, Pearl quickly blocked him, herding him away just as Echo flipped her stone up. Whew! That had been close. She didn't want any of the stones to hit the hatchling. The stones weren't large enough to hurt a dolphin, but Nosy was much smaller.

"Stay right here," she told Nosy. Then she sent a mental image of the little turtle floating in the same spot.

After shooting a worried look toward Riptide, Pearl looked for another stone. She swam extra slowly in case Nosy dashed in front of her again.

"You'd better hurry up, Pearl," Echo warned as she swam past. "You haven't even flipped one stone yet! You don't want Riptide to notice and get mad."

"I know. But Nosy . . ." Pearl began. But then she stopped, since Echo had already zipped away.

Just then Riptide swam toward her. "What's going on over here?" he demanded. "Are you having trouble, Pearl?"

"Um, sort of," Pearl admitted. "I'm sorry. It's just that Nosy is so tiny, and I'm worried that I might hit him with a stone."

"Hmm, I see." Pearl expected Riptide to get annoyed. Instead, he chuckled. "Well, I certainly don't want your cute little pet getting hurt, Pearl. Why don't you just watch today? You can help me judge which of your classmates tosses their stones the highest."

"Oh!" Pearl was surprised and relieved. "Um, okay, sure. Thanks. Come on, Nosy— let's get out of the way."

She guided Nosy to the edge of the class area. The two of them watched the others work on the exercise. Splash, Flip, and most of the others were doing fine. Their stones tumbled higher and higher each time.

But Echo seemed to be having trouble.

Pearl noticed her friend looking toward her several times. Once when she did, her fins got tangled up and she accidentally tossed the stone right at Wiggle.

"Hey!" he exclaimed, dodging aside just in time. "Watch it, Echo!"

Riptide swam toward them. "What's the problem?" he said. "Echo, focus!"

"I'm trying." Echo sounded upset. "I'll do better, I promise."

She didn't hit anyone else with her stones after that. But she still seemed distracted. By the end of class, Pearl was worried. Echo definitely wasn't acting like herself today. Was something wrong?

When Riptide dismissed the class, she swam toward Echo. Halfway there, Bubbles intercepted her.

"I'm glad Nosy is staying all day," Bubbles said with a giggle. "He's so cute!"

Nosy seemed to guess she was talking about him. He swam over and bumped Bubbles on the head with his nose.

"Aw, did you see that?" Harmony swam closer. "He likes you, Bubbles!"

This time Nosy bumped Harmony. Then he zipped away with a chirp.

"I think he wants to play tag," Pearl told them with a smile.

"I'll play!" Splash swam over and tapped the tiny turtle with his fin. "You're it, Nosy!"

Flip and the other boys in the class swam over to join in. They all played tag the whole way back to the school cove. The only one missing was Echo. She was swimming ahead, not looking back at the game.

That made Pearl more worried than ever. Echo loved playing tag. Was she upset about something? Pearl had been so late that morning that the two of them hadn't really talked all day.

Luckily, recess was next. Pearl was sure she'd be able to talk to her friend then.

But when Pearl swam into the cove, Echo was nowhere in sight. Lots of other students were hanging around, though. Finny and his friends swam over when they saw Nosy.

"Can we play with him?" Finny asked.

"Sure," Pearl said. "We were just playing tag."

"Let's play sparkle tag instead," Shelly suggested. She sang a few notes, at the same time sending a burst of beautiful magical sparkles floating out into the water.

Nosy's eyes widened when he saw the sparkles. He darted forward, snapping at the dancing lights as if he were trying to eat them.

Mullet shouted with laughter. "He's awesome!" he exclaimed. "Here, little dude—chase this!"

He created more magical sparkles. His weren't as fancy as Shelly's, but Nosy still loved them. Pearl was glad that Mullet was acting so nice. Sometimes he could be mean, especially to the younger dolphins. But she guessed that even a meanie couldn't resist a cute baby turtle!

Before Pearl knew it, at least half the school seemed to be coming over to play with Nosy. But she was afraid to leave him, in case he got scared or overwhelmed around so many dolphins. That meant she couldn't go and look for Echo.

Oh well, she told herself, watching with a smile as Nosy chased Finny around in a circle. *I'll have to talk to her after school.*

After school, Pearl and her friends gathered outside the reef. "I wish Nosy could come to school every day," Splash said with a laugh. "He's fun!"

Nosy chirped and bumped Splash with his nose. Pearl and Flip laughed as Splash chased the tiny turtle around. But Echo just blew out a bubbly snort and turned away.

"Hey, what's wrong, Echo?" Flip asked. "You've been acting weird all day."

Pearl nodded. "I noticed, too," she added, suddenly feeling worried again. "Is everything okay?"

"Sure." Echo stopped and turned to face them. "At least, it will be soon."

"What do you mean?" Splash stopped chasing Nosy, looking confused.

Echo glanced at Nosy. "I decided something," she announced. "Since Pearl has a pet turtle now, I'm going to find myself a cool pet, too!"

5

Echo's Pet

PEARL WAS SURPRISED BY WHAT ECHO HAD said. "A pet?" she echoed. "But Nosy isn't my pet. He's my friend."

"What's the difference?" Echo sounded distracted. She was staring around thoughtfully. "Now I just have to figure out what kind of pet I want . . ."

She swam away before her friends could say anything else. "That was weird," Splash said. "I wonder why she suddenly decided she needs a pet."

"Who knows, who cares." Flip nudged

Nosy with his snout. "Let's play tag on our way home. Nosy, you're it!"

By the time Pearl got to school the next morning, she'd almost forgotten what Echo had said. That was because all her focus was on Nosy—who had followed her to school again! No matter what she said or how much guiding she used, she couldn't convince him to stay home.

"Hey, it's Nosy!" Splash cried when Pearl swam into the cove with the little turtle right behind her.

Bay was there, too. "Show and Tell was yesterday, remember?" she told Pearl with a smile.

"I'm sorry," Pearl said as more dolphins gathered around. "I couldn't get him to stay at home! My dad said he'll come get him at recess. Is it okay if he stays here until then?"

"Of course," Bay said.

After she swam away, the students started playing with Nosy. Splash's brother was teaching him how to do a somersault when Echo and Flip arrived.

"Sorry we're late!" Echo called out. "I had to go slowly so my new pet could keep up."

"Yeah." Flip didn't sound happy. "He's really slow."

Pearl was surprised to see a spiny lobster following Echo. "Hey, cool," Finny said, swimming closer for a better look. "I like his spots."

"Thanks!" Echo sounded pleased. "I decided to call him Beauty, since he's so pretty."

"That's a good name," Shelly agreed. Then she giggled as Nosy bumped her with his nose. "Oops, Nosy wants to play! Tag, you're it, little cutie!"

She dashed off with the baby turtle chasing her. Echo frowned.

"Why is that turtle here again?" she asked.

Pearl shrugged. "He liked school so much yesterday that he wanted to come back," she explained. "Don't worry, he won't be here all day."

"Good." Echo blew out a narrow stream of bubbles. "He's pretty distracting."

Pearl didn't think that was a very nice thing to say. But she didn't want to argue with her best friend. "Where did you find Beauty?" she asked instead.

"Near my pod's reef," Echo replied. "He's great, isn't he? He's probably the most interesting pet I could have, right?"

"Sure, I guess." Pearl was distracted when Nosy zipped past, almost bumping into her. "Slow down, Nosy! You're going to crash into something!"

"So what if he does?" Mullet said with a laugh. "He's got his shell to protect him."

"Be careful," Echo exclaimed as Finny

dodged away from Nosy and almost bumped into her.

"Look out, Echo," Shelly warned. "Your lobster is getting away."

Sure enough, Beauty was scuttling off across the sandy seafloor. A second later he disappeared beneath a section of reef.

"Hey!" Echo exclaimed. "Get back out here, Beauty."

She sent out a burst of magical energy. "Are you guiding him?" Pearl asked.

"Of course. How do you think I got him here?" Echo sent out another magical burst. Finally Beauty peeped out from his hiding place.

"It's time for Music class," Flip said. "We should go."

"Hold on. He's coming . . ." Echo said.

"Here, I'll help." Pearl touched her friend's fin and focused on combining her own magical energy with Echo's. That made the magic stronger.

Even working together, it took them a few minutes to get the lobster to come out. By then the rest of their school pod had gone to class. Even Nosy had followed the boys.

"Hurry," Echo said. "Help me guide Beauty to Music, okay?"

"Sure." Pearl couldn't help thinking that Echo was being kind of bossy—both to Beauty, and to Pearl herself! But Pearl liked to help her friends, so she touched Echo's fin again and focused her energy on the spiny lobster. Finally they convinced him to go with them.

When they arrived, Bay was about to start

class. "Sorry we're late," Pearl said.

"Yeah," Echo added. "Pearl was helping me guide my new pet here. He's, um, a little stubborn."

"I see." Bay gazed at Beauty thoughtfully. "And yes, spiny lobsters tend to swim to their own tune." She glanced at Echo. "You shouldn't be offended if he decides to leave again."

"Oh, he won't." Echo sounded confident.

Beauty stuck around for the first few minutes of class. Then Bay asked Echo to sing her homework assignment. Within a few notes, Beauty started scuttling away again.

"Watch out!" Pearl blurted out. "He's—oh. Too late."

The spiny lobster was gone. This time he'd hidden in a crevice in the reef.

Echo stopped singing. "I'd better get him out of there," she said. "Here, Beauty . . ."

She sent several bursts of magical energy toward the reef. But there was no sign of Beauty.

Echo frowned. "He's not responding," she complained. "Maybe I need to try pushing him."

"No," Bay said firmly. "Pushing is for emergencies only."

Pearl nodded. She was surprised that her friend would even think about using magical pushing on her new pet. Pushing was sort of like guiding, except that it *forced* a creature to do as a dolphin said instead of just *asking*. As Bay had said, it was only supposed to be used in an emergency.

"Maybe he'll come out on his own," Pearl said.

Echo scowled. "I doubt it," she muttered. "He's probably too stubborn to be a good pet, anyway. I'll just have to find a different one—an even better one."

Recess was about half over when Pearl's father swam into the cove. "Hello," he sang out cheerfully. "Any baby turtles here for me to take home?"

"Aw, does he have to go?" Splash was playing tag with Nosy. "He's so much fun!"

"Sorry." Pearl's dad smiled at him. "School is for learning, not for playing. Come on, Nosy."

The little turtle chirped, sounding disappointed. But he followed Pearl's dad out of the school.

"Bye, Nosy!" several students called.

Pearl was sorry to see the turtle go. But she was also relieved. Now she wouldn't have to worry about where he was and what he was doing all the time.

She looked around for her friends. Splash and Flip were nearby. But there was no sign of Echo.

"Where's Echo?" she asked the boys.

Flip looked around. "She was with us when we left Jumping and Swimming."

"I haven't seen her since then," Splash put in.

"Hey, everyone!" Echo's excited cry rang out.

Then she swam into the cove with a large horseshoe crab!

6

Memory Test

"WHOA!" SPLASH DODGED AS THE CRAB'S long, spiky tail almost poked him. "Watch where you're pointing that thing!"

Echo giggled. "Isn't she cool? Her name is Spike."

"That's a good name for her." Flip stared at the crab. "Where'd you find her?"

"Over that way." Echo waved a fin at the school entrance. "Right at the edge of Bigsky Basin."

"Bigsky Basin?" Pearl gasped. "You mean you went there just now—by yourself?"

"Maybe she wanted to find a big bull shark for a pet," Splash joked.

Pearl didn't think his joke was very funny. Bigsky Basin could be dangerous! How could Echo have gone there without even telling anyone?

"There were no sharks there." Echo sounded annoyed. "Anyway, don't you guys have anything else to say about my new pet?"

Just then Finny, Shelly, and Mullet swam over. "Hey, is that a horseshoe crab?" Finny exclaimed. "Cool!"

"Thanks." Echo sounded happier. "Her name's Spike. She's my new pet."

"Wow." Shelly sounded impressed as she swam around Spike. "What are you going to do with her?"

"Um . . ." Echo didn't get a chance to answer. Old Salty was announcing the end of recess.

"We'd better get to Ocean Lore," Pearl said. "Are you going to bring Spike?"

"Of course!" Echo said. "I'm sure Old Salty will want to see her."

But Old Salty barely glanced at the horseshoe crab when Echo introduced her. "A new pet, hmm?" he said. Then he cleared his throat. "Settle down, young scholars! It's time for a pop quiz."

"What?" Flip sounded surprised. "You

didn't tell us we were having a quiz today!"

Old Salty chuckled. "That's what makes it a pop quiz," he said. "It will test how closely you were paying attention at Show and Tell yesterday. I want to know whether you all learned anything from one another."

That sounded sort of interesting to Pearl. She just hoped she remembered everything. Having Nosy around had been a little distracting.

The quiz began. Old Salty called on the students one at a time, asking each of them to talk about one of the items a classmate had brought for Show and Tell. When it was Pearl's turn, he asked what she remembered about the pipefish Bubbles had brought. Pearl told him everything she could remember.

"Very good," the teacher said. "Harmony?

You're next. Please tell me about Pearl's Show and Tell creature."

"Oh, that's easy!" Harmony said eagerly. "She brought a baby sea turtle." She quickly repeated everything Pearl had told them about Nosy and his fellow turtles. Even then, Harmony wasn't finished. "I also asked my pod about sea turtles after school," she said. "They told me turtles have to breathe air from above the surface, just like we dolphins do. And some of them can live to be eighty years old!"

By the time she finished talking about turtles, Old Salty was nodding and smiling.

"Excellent, Harmony!" he exclaimed. "I'm so glad that our Show and Tell exercise inspired you to learn more."

"Thanks." Harmony smiled at Pearl. "It's mostly because Pearl brought such an interesting creature. Thanks, Pearl."

"You're welcome." Pearl smiled back.

Old Salty called on Flip next. He did fine, and so did most of the other students. Finally it was Echo's turn.

"Echo, please tell me about what Splash brought for Show and Tell," the teacher said.

"Um . . ." Echo looked blank. She glanced at her horseshoe crab, who was drifting away. "Hey, Spike, get back here!"

"Echo?" Old Salty said once Spike was beside Echo again. "We're waiting."

"Sorry." Echo shot another look at Spike. Then she cleared her throat. "Um, did Splash bring the Land Legger thingy?"

"Right!" Splash said, doing a quick flip.

"Can you tell me more about it?" Old Salty prompted.

"It was, um, sort of clear and hard? I don't really—ouch!"

Spike had just turned around, accidentally poking Echo with her pointy tail. A few students giggled.

Old Salty just sighed. "All right, Echo," he said. "Please try to pay better attention next time. I don't expect everyone to do extra research like Harmony." He smiled at Harmony. "But I know you can do better than this."

Echo's fins slumped, and she nodded. "Sorry, Old Salty," she said in a soft voice.

Pearl felt sorry for her friend. Echo usually did well in all her classes. But not lately. First she'd messed up in Magic, then in Jumping and Swimming, and now this! No wonder poor Echo had been acting a little bossy and grumpy lately—she was having a terrible week!

7

In the Lagoon

"Hey, where's Spike?" Splash asked as the four friends swam out of the cove after school.

"I let her go during Magic class." Echo sighed. "It was too hard guiding her to stay."

Pearl rubbed her friend's fin. "That's okay," she said. "You don't really need to have a pet around all the time, right?"

"Actually, I was hoping to find something better," Echo said. "Can I swim you home, Pearl?"

"Are you hoping to get Nosy to be your pet?" Flip teased.

Echo frowned. "Of course not," she said. "But Pearl's lagoon is far away. Maybe there will be more interesting pets there."

Pearl wasn't sure what to say. She wished Echo wasn't so determined to find herself a pet. But she didn't want to tell her she couldn't come to the lagoon.

"Okay, let's go," she said. "I'm sure Squeak and my parents will be happy to see you."

"Can I come, too?" Splash asked eagerly. "I want to say hi to Nosy."

"Me too," Flip put in. "You said there are other baby turtles there, too, right? Can we play with them?"

"Sure," Pearl said, feeling better already. Maybe Echo would have so much fun playing with the tiny turtles that she'd forget all about trying to find a pet!

When they arrived in the lagoon, Pearl's parents weren't there. Squeak explained that they'd gone to help a fish who was tangled in some Land Legger string.

"But I can show you around!" Squeak told Pearl's friends eagerly. "Come on, let's see the beach first . . ."

She gave Echo, Splash, and Flip a tour. Along the way, Nosy and some of the other baby turtles joined the group.

Pearl could tell that Flip and Splash were having lots of fun with the hatchlings. The two dolphins played tag with the smaller creatures. They also practiced their guiding and other magical skills to get the turtles to swim in funny patterns. The baby turtles loved that, too!

But Echo wasn't really joining in on the

fun. She kept looking around as they swam through the lagoon. She stopped to stare at a pretty spotted trunkfish, and then swam down to examine an especially large oyster.

"Hey, who's that?" she blurted out as they passed one of the reef formations.

At first Pearl didn't know what she meant. Then she saw movement inside a big hole in the coral.

"Oh, that's Inky," she said. "He's a reef octopus. He lives here in the lagoon."

"He's cool." Echo peered in at the octopus. "Come out and say hi, Inky."

She sent a burst of magical energy toward the octopus. "Careful," Pearl warned. "He can be a little grumpy sometimes."

"Help me bring him out," Echo urged. "Please?"

"Well . . . okay." Pearl sent the octopus a mental message, just like she always did when she and Squeak invited him to come out and play.

At first Inky ignored her. But finally he wiggled out and stared at her.

"Wow, he's cool." Echo swam around the octopus. "I think I just found my new pet!"

"What?" Pearl blurted out. "Echo, no, wait . . ."

But it was too late. Echo was already sending out another burst of magic. Inky backed away—and then sent out a poof of dark ink right in Echo's face!

"Hey!" Echo exclaimed as Inky ducked back into his lair.

"Sorry about that," Pearl said. "I told you he can be grumpy."

She was sure Echo would change her mind about making Inky her pet. But Echo just waved her fins to disperse the ink.

"That's okay—it's really interesting how he can do that, actually," Echo said. She noticed Flip and Splash playing with the baby turtles nearby. "Hey, Flip, come here and help me guide my new pet home!"

Squeak swam over with the boys. "What's going on?" she asked. "Oh, hi, Inky!"

"Echo wants to take Inky home with her," Pearl told her sister.

"What? Why?" Squeak sounded alarmed. "He lives here!"

"Not anymore." Echo focused her magic on Inky. "Come out, Inky-winky! Please?"

Pearl wanted to stop Echo from taking the octopus away. But what could she say? Echo was just guiding him. If Inky wanted to go with her, it wasn't fair to stop him. Right?

It took some extra energy from Flip, but finally Echo convinced Inky to follow her out through the lagoon entrance. Splash said good-bye and swam off, too. A few minutes after that, Pearl's parents finally returned.

"Mom! Dad!" Squeak zipped toward them.

"Inky's gone!"

She and Pearl told their parents what had happened. "Oh dear," their father said when he heard the news.

"Will Inky be okay?" Squeak seemed more upset than ever. "He never leaves the lagoon! What if he never comes back?"

Their parents traded a look. "I'm sure Inky will be fine," Pearl's mother said. "Echo is very smart and responsible."

"Yes, I'm sure she'll take good care of him," their father added. He looked at Pearl. "Do you know why she was so interested in Inky? He can be, um, a little temperamental."

"I tried to tell her that." Pearl sighed out a stream of bubbles. "Maybe she'll get tired of him soon and send him home. I guess we'll just have to see what happens."

8

A Surprise Substitution

PEARL SWAM TO SCHOOL EARLY THE NEXT day. She wanted to be there when Echo arrived with Inky. Her whole family was eager to hear how he was doing in his new home.

But when Echo appeared, the octopus was nowhere in sight. Instead, a large, flat, blue-spotted fish was gliding slowly along between her and Flip.

"Where's Inky?" Pearl asked, dashing forward to meet them. Splash was right behind her. "Hey, is that a peacock flounder?" he asked.

"Yes," Echo replied. "This is my new pet, Gurgle."

"What happened to Inky?" Pearl asked. "I thought he was your new pet."

Echo frowned. "He swam away while I was sleeping," she said. "It's just as well. He inked me twice more on the way home yesterday!"

Pearl let out a burst of worried bubbles. "He hardly ever leaves the lagoon," she said. "I hope he can find his way back by himself."

"Maybe you should send your parents a message to go look for him," Splash suggested.

Flip nodded. "You could ask Bay to help you send it."

"That's a great idea." Pearl was pretty good at sending messages to nearby dolphins, but it took much more energy to send one long distances. She would definitely need an adult to help her with that.

"I'm sure Inky can find his way back just fine," Echo said with a frown. "Anyway, don't you guys want to play with Gurgle?"

"Um, sure." Splash swam closer to the peacock flounder. "He's really big."

"Yeah," Flip agreed. "He's pretty laid-back, too. We had to keep waiting for him to catch up on the way here. But he didn't mind a bit when I dragged him part of the way so we wouldn't be late!"

Pearl felt annoyed. She was worried about Inky, and Echo didn't seem to be thinking much about anyone but herself. For a second Pearl was tempted to say that there were lots of peacock flounders near her home lagoon, so Echo's new pet wasn't really that unique. But she stopped herself. Her father had a favorite saying: *Always choose kindness*. So Pearl decided to be kind instead of mean.

"His spots are really pretty," she told Echo. "I've never seen one that exact shade of blue before."

"Me neither." Echo sounded happy as she glanced at Gurgle. "I think I finally found the coolest pet in the sea! Come on—let's go show everyone else!"

Gurgle was still following Echo around when Pearl and her friends arrived at Jumping and

Swimming class. But Riptide didn't seem to notice the slow-moving fish.

"All right, dolphins!" he barked out. "Today we're going to work on your stamina. I noticed some extra trips up for air yesterday during class."

He explained that they were going to swim all the way to the edge of Bigsky Basin and back again.

"Make sure you all keep up," he ordered. "And no stopping until I say so! Ready? Let's go!"

Pearl wasn't a very fast swimmer. But she did her best to stay with the group. She was surprised when she noticed she was passing Echo, who was usually pretty fast.

"Are you okay?" Pearl called to her friend.

"I'm fine." Echo slowed down even more.

"I'm just staying back so Gurgle can keep up."

Pearl noticed the flounder gliding along well behind the group. "Peacock flounders aren't very fast swimmers," Pearl reminded Echo. "Maybe he should stay behind."

"No!" Echo said quickly. "He'll be fine. Come on, Gurgle."

She sent a burst of magical energy to help the big fish go faster. But he was still way behind everyone else.

A moment later Riptide looked back. "Echo!" he yelled. "Stop dawdling!"

"Sorry!" Echo called. "I need to wait for my pet."

Riptide turned and sped back toward her. "Keep going, everyone!" he called as he passed the other students. "I'll catch up in a moment."

When the teacher reached Echo, Pearl was

still close enough to hear them.

"I can't leave Gurgle behind," Echo explained, sounding upset. "He might wander off!"

"If that fish is your friend, he'll be here when you get back," Riptide told her sternly. "Now go!"

A moment later Echo passed Pearl. "Are you okay?" Pearl called, but her friend didn't answer.

By the time the class made it back to where they'd started, even Splash was tired and out of breath. The only one who still seemed fine was Riptide.

"Good job, class!" he shouted with a smile. "If we do that every day for a week, you might impress me yet!"

Meanwhile, Echo was looking around.

"He's gone," she blurted out. "Oh no! Gurgle is gone!"

When class ended, Pearl hurried to catch up with Echo. "Are you okay?" she asked. "Gurgle seemed to like you. Maybe he'll come back."

"Probably not." Echo sounded upset. "I need to find a new pet. Will you help me?"

"Um, I guess so." Pearl wanted to tell her friend that she didn't need a pet to be happy. In fact, she wanted to say that all the focus on pets seemed to be making Echo *un*happy! But she was afraid that would upset Echo even more, so she didn't say anything. *Always choose kindness*, she thought.

The boys were already back inside the school cove. But Pearl followed Echo out into the sun-dappled water nearby.

"What kind of pet are you looking for this time?" she asked.

"It doesn't matter," Echo replied. "It just has to be cool, that's all." She zipped toward a passing triggerfish. "Maybe that guy . . ."

But the triggerfish swam away as soon as Echo sent magic at it. So did the grouper that she found a few minutes later.

"Recess will be over soon," Pearl said as she watched a shrimp scuttle away under a rock. "Maybe we should go back."

"Not until I find my pet." Echo spotted a school of angelfish drifting along nearby. "Hey, look at that one! Here, fishy fishy . . ."

This time her guiding worked. The largest and prettiest angelfish floated slowly toward her. She was mostly bright yellow, with dramatic blue-and-purple markings.

Echo smiled. "Hi there," she said. "I think I'll call you Sky."

When Pearl, Echo, and the angelfish swam into the cove, Shelly was just inside. "Ooh, what a pretty fish!" she said.

"Her name's Sky," Echo told the older dolphin.

"That's perfect." Shelly sent out a burst of magical lights and bubbles, which danced around the elegant fish. "Look, I made her a frame! She looks even more beautiful now!"

"Yes, she does!" Echo agreed happily. "I think I finally found the perfect pet!"

Pearl just sighed, hoping that Sky would stick around for a while. Maybe then Echo would stop searching for new pets all the time and go back to her normal self.

9

Fast or Slow

PEARL HAD TROUBLE FOCUSING ON WHAT Old Salty was saying during Ocean Lore that day. It was only partly because his lecture was about algae. It was mostly because she was watching Echo and her new pet.

She could tell that Echo was being extra careful not to let Sky swim away. Every few moments, she sent out another burst of magical energy to guide the pretty fish into staying put.

She doesn't get it, Pearl thought. *You can't magically guide another creature into being your friend. Why can't Echo see that?*

Luckily Old Salty didn't notice that some of his students were distracted. Still, Pearl was glad when Ocean Lore was over.

The last class of the day, as always, was Magic. Pearl and her friends were the last ones to arrive, since Sky couldn't swim any faster than Gurgle had.

"Why can't you find a faster pet?" Flip complained as they finally reached the edge of the kelp forest.

The rest of the class was already there. "Hurry over, kids," Bay called. "We have a lot to do today."

Pearl noticed a slender silver barracuda swimming around behind the teacher. She wondered if he was part of that day's lesson.

Bay didn't leave her wondering for long.

"Today we'll be practicing our helping skills," she said. "That's when we use our magic to help another creature do something faster or better."

"Cool," Flip said. "I'm good at that."

Bay smiled at him. "You'll have a chance to prove that in a moment," she said. "We'll all take turns helping this barracuda swim faster."

"I have an idea!" Echo swam forward eagerly. "Maybe some of us can practice on my pet angelfish instead."

"Thanks for the offer, Echo, but I don't think that's a good idea," Bay said firmly. "The barracuda is made to swim in short bursts of speed. By using helping magic, we're aiding his natural abilities." She waved a fin toward Sky. "The angelfish is a much slower swimmer. It's not fair to force her to do something she's not built to do."

"Right," Bubbles called out. "That would be like pushing instead of guiding."

"Yes, exactly." Bay nodded. "Why don't you go first, Pearl?"

Pearl shot a glance toward Echo, who looked unhappy. Then she swam up to take a breath.

When she got back, she focused on the barracuda. Gathering her magical energy, she

sent it toward the slender fish to help him swim faster. But just then, Sky floated out right in front of her.

"Hey!" Pearl cried, quickly trying to stop her magic. "Sky, look out!"

Her magical energy surrounded Sky, sending the angelfish spinning around in circles. Sky sent out a cloud of alarmed bubbles.

"Sorry, Sky!" Pearl exclaimed, sending the fish a mental message. She shot an annoyed look at Echo. "I didn't see you coming."

"It's all right." Bay sent out a burst of guiding energy to help Sky stop spinning, and then to help her float back over toward Echo. "Try it again, Pearl."

Echo was watching Sky. She didn't meet Pearl's eye, and she didn't say she was sorry for letting her pet get in the way. That didn't seem very nice to Pearl. But she did her best to forget about it, and after a quick trip up to the surface for a breath of air, she focused her energy on the barracuda again. This time her helping magic worked, and he zipped across the class area.

"Good!" Bay said. "Let's see if any of your classmates can beat that time."

The next few students fell just short. When Splash took his turn, the barracuda went fast for half the distance, then stopped and turned around.

"Oops," Splash said with a laugh. "Sorry about that. Sky floated past and I got distracted."

Pearl looked over at Echo. Echo didn't apologize to Splash, either. Didn't she care that her pet kept getting in the way?

"That's all right, Splash. You can try again in a moment." Bay looked around. "Flip, it's your turn."

"Good. I'll show everyone how it's done." Flip swam forward. This time the barracuda went faster than ever!

"Awesome!" Splash called out. "You even beat Pearl's time!"

Pearl smiled. "Congratulations, Flip."

"Thanks." Flip grinned. "I told you guys I was good at this!"

Bay chuckled. "There's only one dolphin left to try to beat you," she said. "Echo? You're up."

Echo nodded and looked at Sky. "Stay here," she told the angelfish, sending out a burst of guiding magic.

Then she swam forward and focused on

the barracuda. "Give up now, Echo!" Flip taunted. "You'll never beat me."

"Want to bet?" Echo flashed him a look. Then she turned back to the slender silver fish. "Go, go, go!" she murmured, sending out a strong pulse of energy.

The fish zipped forward—and crossed the class area in the fastest time yet!

"You did it!" Splash cheered. "Great job, Echo!"

Bay nodded, looking impressed. "Excellent work," she told Echo.

"Thanks." Echo smiled. But her smile faded when she turned to where she'd left her pet. "Oh no!" she cried out. "Sky is gone!"

10

Pets or Friends?

"Good job today, Echo," Harmony called out as everyone left at the end of class. "I've never seen a barracuda move that fast!"

"Thanks," Echo called back. Then she looked at her friends and frowned. "I just wish Sky hadn't left. Why do all my pets want to escape?"

Pearl was still feeling annoyed with her friend because of what had happened in class. But she tried not to show it. "Maybe they don't want to be pets," Pearl suggested. "If you just tried to be friends with them . . ."

Splash and Flip nodded, but Echo didn't seem to be listening. "I should probably look for a sea horse next," she said. "They're pretty calm. Although I heard there's a really cool ray hanging around near my pod . . ."

Pearl sighed out a burst of bubbles. "Oh Echo! Aren't you ever going to stop searching for the perfect pet?" she exclaimed.

Echo looked surprised. "What do you mean?"

"She means it's getting boring." Flip poked her with his fin. "All you talk about lately is pets, pets, pets."

Echo swished her fluke and scowled. "I thought you guys wanted to help me," she said. "I thought you were my friends!"

"We are your friends," Pearl told her. "And some of these other creatures could be, too, if you would only—"

Just then, Bay swam up behind them. "Pearl! I almost forgot," the teacher interrupted. "Your father sent me a mental message just before class. He wanted to let you know that your octopus friend made it home safely."

"Really?" Pearl smiled with relief, almost forgetting about Echo for a second. "That's great! Thanks, Bay."

Behind her, Echo let out a surprised chirp. Turning to look, Pearl saw that a large flounder had just bumped into Echo with his head.

"Hey!" Splash exclaimed. "Look, Gurgle is back! He has something in his mouth."

The flat fish dropped the greenish strand he was holding. "Isn't that nice," Bay commented. "He brought you some seaweed."

"Wow, thanks, Gurgle." Echo sounded surprised. "I thought you left for good."

"I told you he might come back," Pearl said. She looked at Bay. "Echo keeps looking for new pets, but most of them leave after a little while."

"I see." Bay looked thoughtful. "Echo, are you sure looking for a pet is a good idea?"

"What do you mean?" Echo asked.

Bay blew out a slow stream of bubbles. "Dolphins are the protectors of the ocean," she reminded Echo. "That means all the sea's creatures are our friends. But that's different from being our pets, or doing everything we want them to do."

"That's what I was trying to say before, Echo," Pearl blurted out as soon as Bay swam away. She touched her friend's fin. "Nosy and the other turtles are my friends, not my pets. Same with Inky. I love spending time with them and helping them in any way they need me to. But if they don't want my help, they don't have to take it."

"Sounds like my friendship with Spinner," Splash spoke up.

Pearl nodded. Not long ago, Splash had helped a young blacktip shark who'd been separated from his family.

Flip laughed. "Yeah. Spinner definitely wasn't your pet!"

Echo looked angry for a second. "But I just . . ." Suddenly she stopped and looked sheepish. "Oh. Okay, I think I get it," she said. "Sorry if I've been a pain in the snout lately."

"You were," Flip said with a laugh.

"But it's okay," Pearl added quickly. "I just don't understand why you wanted a pet so much."

Echo shrugged. "I guess I thought a really cool pet would make me special, just like you guys."

Pearl traded a surprised look with Splash and Flip. "What do you mean?" she said. "You *are* special, Echo!"

"Yeah." Splash nodded. "Everyone knows you're the best in our whole class at magic."

"Not when I tried to guide that conger eel," Echo reminded him. "You did much better than me at that." She sighed. "Just like Harmony was better at Old Salty's quiz yesterday. And of course Pearl was the best at Show and Tell . . ."

Suddenly Pearl understood what her friend was feeling. "Oh, Echo," she blurted out. "I know you're used to being the best at lots of stuff. And this week, well, I guess you haven't been."

"That's what I just said." Echo sighed out a thick stream of bubbles.

"But everyone has a bad day—or a bad week—sometimes," Pearl said. "It doesn't mean you're not special."

"Yeah." Splash rubbed Echo's fin with his. "Anyway, you're *always* awesome at being our friend!"

"That's right," Pearl said.

Flip nodded. "Uh-huh."

"Really?" Echo smiled uncertainly. "So you guys still like me—even when I'm having a bad week? When I'm—when I'm not the best?"

"Of course!" all three of them chorused. "Don't be such a jellyfish," Flip added with a snort.

Pearl laughed, relieved that Echo was sounding more like herself again. "Now do we have to go searching for another pet?" she teased.

"No way." Echo laughed, too. Then she looked at the peacock flounder, who was still floating nearby. "You don't have to stick around, Gurgle."

"Come on, we'll all swim you home," Splash told her.

Pearl nodded. She followed as her friends

headed out. Then she noticed something.

"Look," she said. "Gurgle is coming with us!"

"Really?" Echo turned and smiled at the fish. "Hey, maybe I really did finally find a really cool . . . er, *not* pet. *Friend*."

"Maybe," Pearl said slowly. Did this mean that Echo was still thinking about trying to impress everyone?

"Don't worry, Pearl." Echo rubbed her fin. "Even if Gurgle swims away halfway home, it's okay. Because I just remembered something."

"What?" Splash asked.

Echo laughed, sending bubbles spurting up toward the sunlit surface of the Salty Sea. "I remembered that I'm *always* the best at one thing—having the coolest, best, most amazing friends in the entire ocean!"

Don't miss the next
adventure at

Pearl's Perfect Gift

'Tis the season of the Sea Solstice, the biggest dolphin
holiday of the year! Pearl wants to give her favorite teacher,
Bay, an extra-special gift. But every time she comes up with
a great idea, another dolphin beats her to the punch! Can Pearl
figure out the perfect gift before the celebration is over?